Finding Out About
THINGS
AT HOME

Written by: **Eliot Humberstone**
Designed by: **Iain Ashman and Sarah Simpson**

Consultant **Betty**
Editor **Root**
Science **Anthony**
Consultant: **Wilson**

Researcher:
Judy Allen
Illustrated by:
Basil Arm
Louise Nevett
Sarah Simpson
Graham Smith

Contents

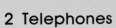

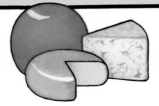

How a telephone works

1 Every telephone has its own number. When you dial a number, an electric message tells the telephone exchange which phone to ring.

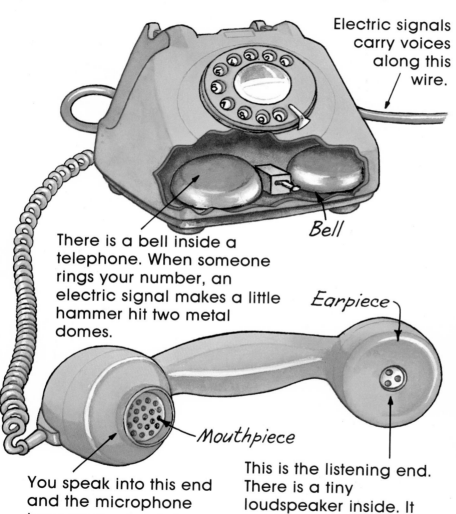

Electric signals carry voices along this wire.

There is a bell inside a telephone. When someone rings your number, an electric signal makes a little hammer hit two metal domes.

Bell

Earpiece

Mouthpiece

You speak into this end and the microphone turns your voice into an electric signal.

This is the listening end. There is a tiny loudspeaker inside. It can turn electric signals back into sounds.

2

HELLO

When you speak, the air from your mouth shakes the air around you. Each sound shakes the air in a different way.

5

At the telephone exchange, machines send the signals to the phone number you want.

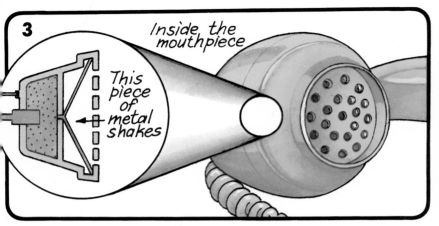

Inside the mouthpiece

This piece of metal shakes ←

There is a thin piece of metal in a telephone mouthpiece. Each word you say shakes it in a different way. It is this part of a microphone that changes sounds into electrical signals.

Electric signals which carry voices go along wires to a telephone exchange.

Underwater cable

Wires at the bottom of the sea or satellites up in the sky carry telephone signals over long distances.

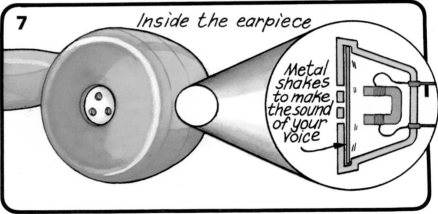

Inside the earpiece

Metal shakes to make the sound of your voice ←

In the earpiece of a telephone is a loudspeaker. Electric signals make the magnet in a loudspeaker pull and release a metal plate. The metal shaking makes the sound of the other person's voice.

How a television works

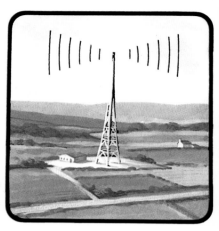

The picture you see on your TV is filmed by a special camera. This can be a long way away. The camera turns pictures into an electric signal. The microphone picks up sound which is turned into more electric signals.

The signals go along a cable to a TV transmitter. Pictures and words are sent out through the air like invisible messages.

A TV will not work well without an aerial. It can be fixed on to the roof of your house, or a small one can stand on the TV. The aerial picks up messages from the transmitter and sends them to the TV set.

When you switch on your set, it turns the signals in the wire back into sound and pictures.

Inside a television

The signal from the television transmitter is picked up by the aerial. It goes through a wire to the inside of the set.

The weak signal is made stronger in the amplifier.

The picture part of the signal goes into three electron guns. These point beams of electricity at the back of the screen.

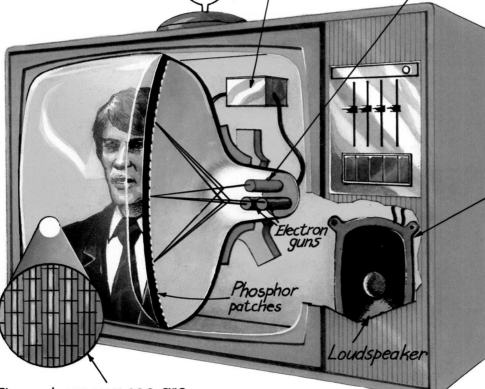

Aerial

Electron guns

Phosphor patches

Loudspeaker

The sound part of the signal goes to the loudspeaker. It changes electricity back into sound.

The colours you see are made up of tiny patches of red, blue and green. They are so small that they merge together when you look at them.

The back of the screen is covered with thousands of tiny patches of a chemical called phosphor. When electricity hits this phosphor, the patches glow red, blue or green.

5

How bread is made

Bread is made from the seeds of the wheat plant. Wheat grows where there is plenty of sun and rain.

When the wheat is ripe, it is cut by a combine harvester. It is then sent to a flour mill.

At the mill, machines crush the wheat into a fine powder called flour.

At the bakers

First the dough is mixed in a mixing machine.

This person is making the pieces of dough into loaves.

This woman is cutting dough into loaf-sized pieces.

6

To make bread, you mix fat, salt, water and yeast with the flour. This makes a dough.

The yeast makes the dough rise. When it has risen, it is put into a hot oven to bake.

The dough turns into bread after being baked for about an hour. It is taken out and left to cool.

The loaves are put on trays and then they are put in the oven to bake.

The fresh bread is ready to be taken to the shop.

The loaves are left on racks to rise. Bowls of water below help keep the air damp.

Milk and cheese

1 Most milk comes from cows. Cows can only make milk if they eat enough fresh grass and drink enough water. Cows drink about 60 litres of water a day.

2 A cow makes milk to feed her calf. The calf sucks milk from a teat on the cow's udder.

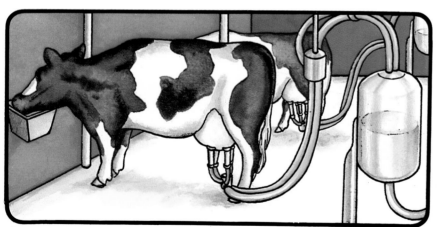

3 The milk we drink is taken from the cow by a machine. This sucks the milk out. The milk goes into a tank to be cooled. Often the cow eats food while she is being milked.

4 A tanker takes milk from the farm to the dairy. The tanker is insulated to keep the milk cool.

5 When the tanker arrives at the dairy, the milk is unloaded. It is pumped out through a long hose.

6 Most milk is pasteurized. This means it is heated up and then cooled down quickly. This kills all the germs.

7 The pasteurized milk is put into bottles or cartons. Now it is ready for people to buy.

How cheese is made

Cheese is made from milk. It is mixed with rennet, a chemical from the lining of a cow's stomach.

The rennet makes the milk into a thick curd. Salt is added and the curd is packed into moulds.

The curd is stored in a cool place. After about four months, it turns into cheese.

Cameras and films

The film is inside the case

Window

Film is kept inside a plastic case. This kind of case has a square window in the middle. Light can only get to the part of the film which is in the window.

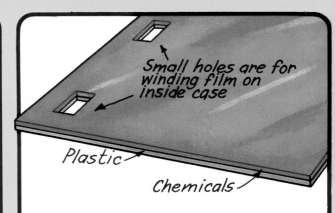

Small holes are for winding film on inside case

Plastic

Chemicals

The film is made of very thin plastic. It is covered on one side with chemicals. When light shines on the chemicals, it makes an invisible picture on the film.

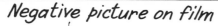
Negative picture on film

After you have finished taking your film, you send it to be developed. Developed film looks like this. The picture is called a negative because it is the opposite of the photograph you will get in the end.

You put the negatives in here

You put a negative film into an enlarger and shine light through it on to a piece of photographic paper. This makes the finished photograph.

Inside a camera

1 The picture below shows a simple camera. It is cut away so that you can see how it works.

2 You press this button to take a picture. It makes a shutter open and close. The shutter is a small metal plate behind the lens.

You wind on the film after you have taken a picture. A new piece of film is then in the window of the case.

3 The shutter opens for a moment and lets in light. Then it closes again. When the light shines in, it makes an invisible picture on the film.

4 This is the lens, it is a curved piece of glass. This makes light rays from in front of the camera make a clear picture on the film at the back of the camera.

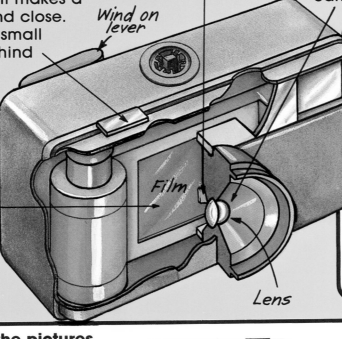

Wind on lever

Film

Lens

What the lens does to light

With a magnifying glass, you can use light from a window to make an upside-down picture like a camera lens does.

After taking the pictures

When you have used up all the film, you have to take it out of the camera. Some films take 12 and some take as many as 36 pictures.

Film case goes in here

To take the film out, you open up the back of the camera. Then you send the film away to be developed and printed.

Light bulbs and torches

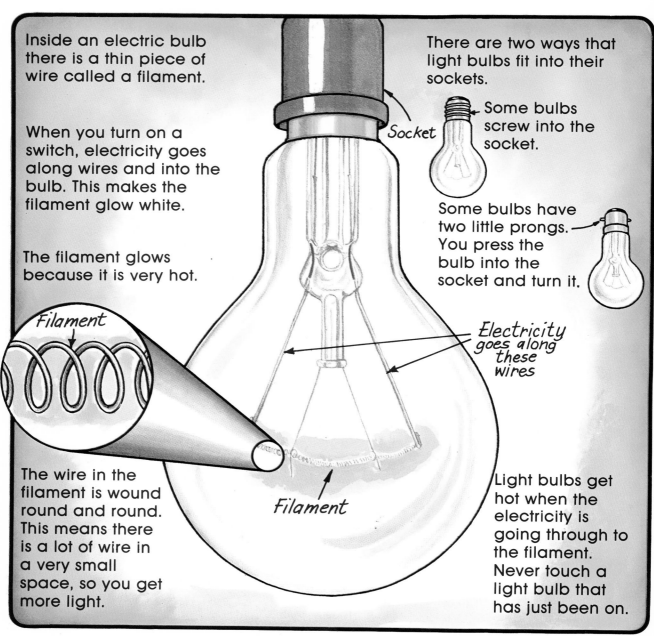

Inside an electric bulb there is a thin piece of wire called a filament.

When you turn on a switch, electricity goes along wires and into the bulb. This makes the filament glow white.

The filament glows because it is very hot.

Filament

The wire in the filament is wound round and round. This means there is a lot of wire in a very small space, so you get more light.

There are two ways that light bulbs fit into their sockets.

Socket

Some bulbs screw into the socket.

Some bulbs have two little prongs. You press the bulb into the socket and turn it.

Electricity goes along these wires

Filament

Light bulbs get hot when the electricity is going through to the filament. Never touch a light bulb that has just been on.

Inside a torch

Torches work like ordinary lights in your home. They use electricity from the batteries inside.

Inside a battery there are chemicals that make electricity.

The torch only lights up if the electricity flows through both batteries. It goes to the bulb and back to the bottom of the batteries again. That is why there are strips of metal in the sides of the torch for the electricity to flow along.

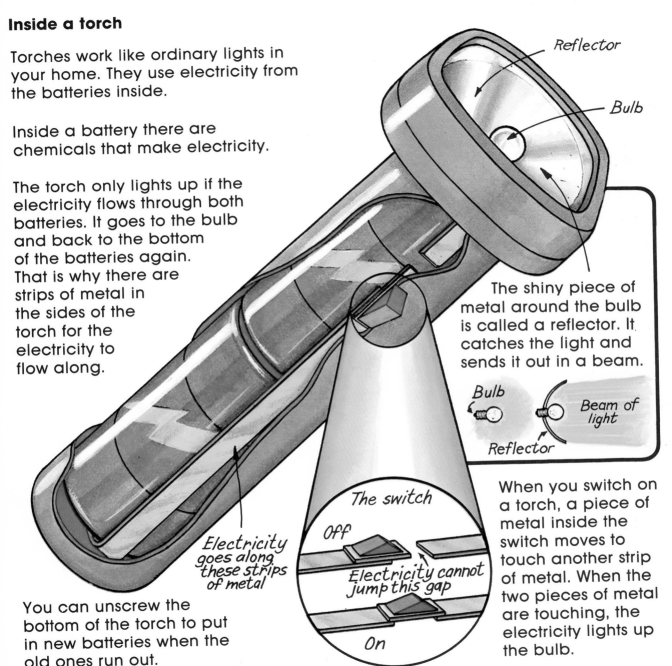

Reflector

Bulb

The shiny piece of metal around the bulb is called a reflector. It catches the light and sends it out in a beam.

Bulb

Beam of light

Reflector

Electricity goes along these strips of metal

The switch

Off

Electricity cannot jump this gap

On

You can unscrew the bottom of the torch to put in new batteries when the old ones run out.

When you switch on a torch, a piece of metal inside the switch moves to touch another strip of metal. When the two pieces of metal are touching, the electricity lights up the bulb.

13

How a cooker works

Not all cookers use electricity to make them hot. The one above uses coal. The one below uses gas.

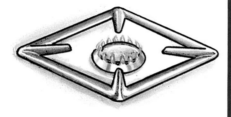

You can cook food out of doors on a barbecue grill. Barbecues burn charcoal which is made from partly burnt wood.

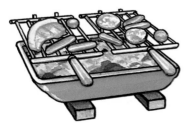

How an electric cooker works

Inside the metal rings on top of an electric cooker, there is a wire called an element. When you turn on the cooker, electricity goes through the element. This makes the element very hot. There is a special powder around the element to stop the electricity getting to the metal ring.

Element

Powder

Electric cookers have a thermostat connected to the oven switch. When the oven is hot enough, the thermostat turns off the electricity.

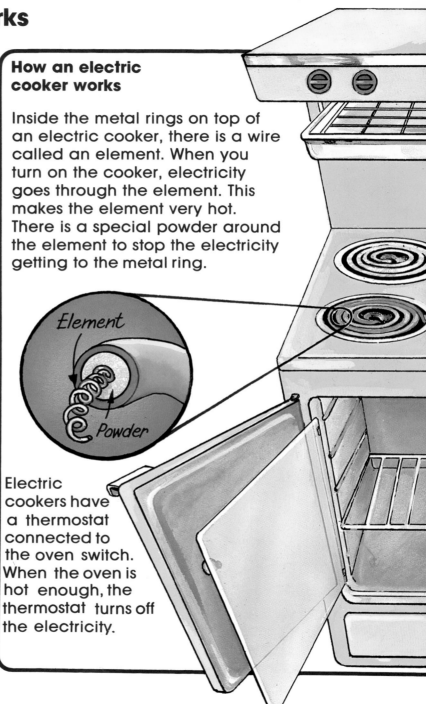

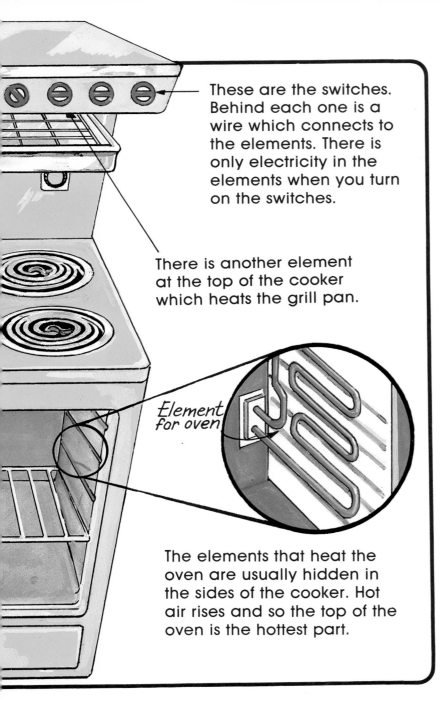

These are the switches. Behind each one is a wire which connects to the elements. There is only electricity in the elements when you turn on the switches.

There is another element at the top of the cooker which heats the grill pan.

Element for oven

The elements that heat the oven are usually hidden in the sides of the cooker. Hot air rises and so the top of the oven is the hottest part.

The earliest way of cooking food was to put it on an open fire.

Before cookers were invented, people used to cook food in pots over fires.

The most modern electric cookers are called microwave cookers. They can bake a potato in about two minutes.

Keeping things cold

Everywhere around us there are thousands of tiny living things, too small for you to see. If you leave food out in the air they start to grow on it and you can see them as mould.

These tiny living things do not like the cold. We put food in the fridge to help stop it going bad.

In the past, ice was used to keep food cool. Farmers made ice by flooding their fields in winter. The fields froze and they collected the ice.

People used to keep food in larders. These were small rooms with cold stone floors. These helped keep the food cool so it stayed fresh longer.

Inside a refrigerator

1 Refrigerators keep things cold because they push the warm air out at the back.

Warm air comes out at the back

2 Fridges are airtight to help keep out warm air. A fridge door must not be left open.

3 At the back there are lots of pipes.

4 Inside the pipes is a liquid. The liquid turns to gas as it goes along the pipes. When it does this, it takes away the heat from the food in the fridge. This makes the food cooler.

5 The gas goes into this compressor. It is then turned into a liquid. Heat comes out when the gas turns to liquid. You can sometimes feel the heat at the back of the fridge.

6 Now the liquid is ready to go through the pipes again and take away more heat from the food.

7 When the food is cool enough, a thermostat switches the compressor off until it is needed again.

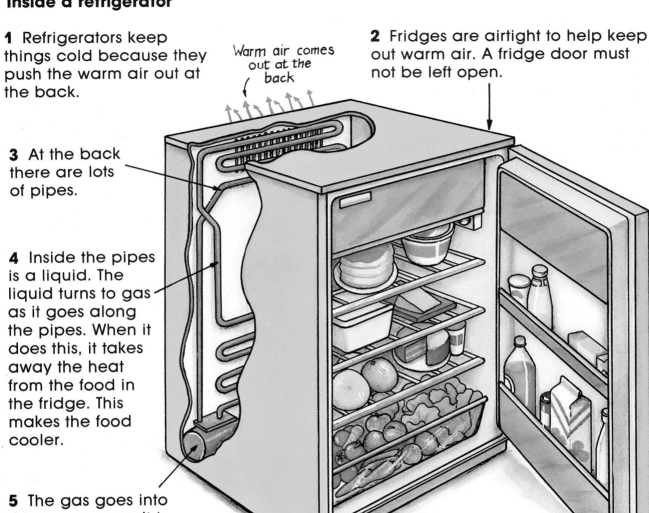

Watches

Inside a watch there are lots of small wheels. After you wind up the watch, a spring unwinds and makes the wheels go round. The hour hand is attached to a wheel that goes round twice a day. The minute hand is joined to a faster wheel that goes round once an hour.

The numbers are stuck on a piece of tin. This goes between the wheels and the glass.

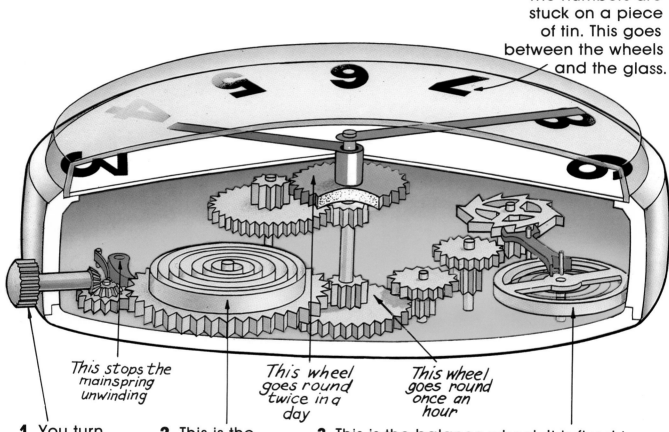

This stops the mainspring unwinding

This wheel goes round twice in a day

This wheel goes round once an hour

1 You turn this knob to wind up the mainspring.

2 This is the mainspring. As it unwinds, it turns round the wheel to which it is attached.

3 This is the balance wheel. It is fixed to a spring that makes it go backwards and forwards. As the balance wheel turns, it makes the lever keep the escape wheel going round at a steady speed.

Inside a digital watch

Digital watches do not have moving hands. They show the time with changing numbers. Instead of springs and wheels, they work by using electricity from a tiny battery. This goes through a tiny quartz crystal and makes it shake over 30,000 times a second.

An electronic counter counts how many times the crystal shakes. Because the crystal shakes at a very even speed, the counter can work out how many seconds, minutes and hours are going by. It can then make the digits change so they show the right time.

1 This battery sends electricity to the tiny quartz crystal.

Electric messages go along these wires

2 Electricity makes the quartz crystal shake very fast.

3 Electronic counter counts how many times the crystal shakes and sends an electric message to the watch face.

How the numbers are made

On some digital watches you can see very faint figures of 8.

The lines are made of a special material that goes dark when electricity comes to it. Each message from the electronic counter makes different lines go dark so you see different numbers every minute.

Try arranging seven matchsticks and you will see how you can make any number from 0 to 9.

Water, taps and toilets

The water we use comes from rain. The rain soaks into the ground and runs into lakes and rivers.

Water is collected from rivers and stored in huge artificial lakes called reservoirs.

Clean water comes in here   *Dirty water comes out here*

After it is cleaned, water from the reservoir comes through pipes under the ground into your home.

How taps work

Taps are joined to metal pipes in the walls. Inside the tap there is a rubber washer. When you turn on the tap the washer comes up.

When the washer is up, water can flow out of the pipe. When you turn off the tap the washer goes down and stops water coming out of the pipe.

The washer is up, so the tap is on

The washer is down, so the tap is off

Washer

Washer

Water from drains goes to pipes underground. These pipes go to sewage works.

At the sewage works, water is cleaned with chemicals. It can now go back into the rivers.

After it has gone into the rivers, water can be collected in the reservoirs and used again.

What happens when you flush the toilet?

The tank above a toilet is called a cistern. It holds the water which is flushed into the bowl when you push the handle down. After it is flushed, the cistern fills with water again.

When you push the handle down, the plunger in the cistern forces water into the bowl below. The ballcock that floats on the water goes down. This makes more water go into the cistern.

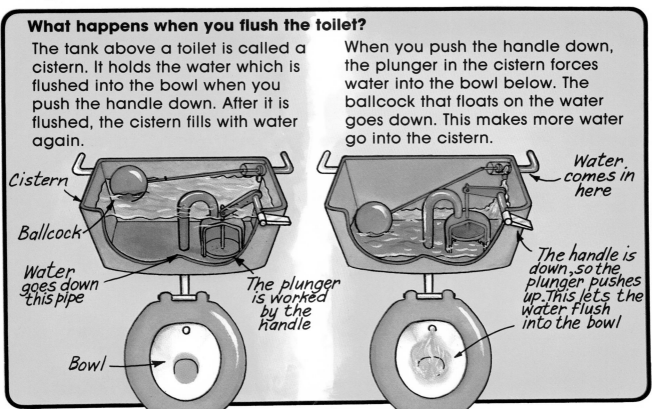

Cistern

Ballcock

Water goes down this pipe

The plunger is worked by the handle

Water comes in here

The handle is down, so the plunger pushes up. This lets the water flush into the bowl

Bowl

Dust and vacuum cleaners

Almost everywhere you go, there is dust in the air. You can sometimes see the dust particles floating in a room when the sun shines through a window. Dust makes things dirty.

Dust test

Every Saturday for four weeks put a sheet of paper somewhere it will collect dust.

4 Weeks   2 Weeks
   3 Weeks   1 Week

At the end of the fourth week, see how much dust you have.

What is dust?

There are lots of different things in dust. You can see some of them in the circle.

These things can be tiny bits of wool and cotton, people's hair, little pieces of skin or the stuffing from chairs.

Sometimes dirt from outside can be found in dust inside.

This is what dust may look like under a microscope.

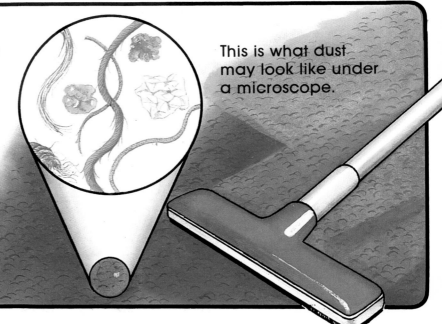

How a vacuum cleaner works

1 Vacuum cleaners work by sucking air in through a tube at one end. Dust, fluff and tiny pieces of material are sucked in with the air.

2 The air with the dust in it goes into the cleaner. The dust stays in a bag and clean air is blown out of the vacuum cleaner.

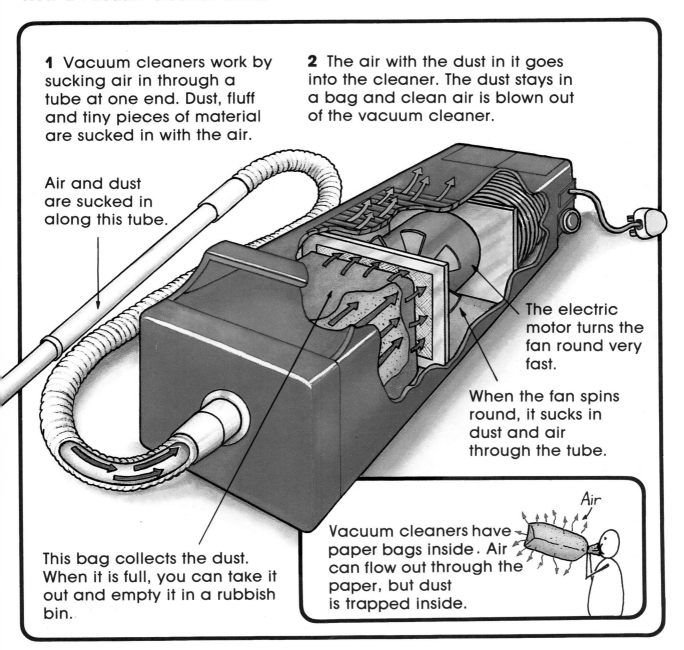

Air and dust are sucked in along this tube.

The electric motor turns the fan round very fast.

When the fan spins round, it sucks in dust and air through the tube.

This bag collects the dust. When it is full, you can take it out and empty it in a rubbish bin.

Vacuum cleaners have paper bags inside. Air can flow out through the paper, but dust is trapped inside.

Air

How glass is made

Old glass can also be mixed with the sand

Furnace

Glass is made from a special kind of sand called silica sand. It is often dug out of quarries.

The sand is mixed with other chemicals made from rocks. Then it is poured into a large furnace. The sand mixture is heated until it is so hot that it melts. It is called molten glass and is like soft toffee.

Furnace

Hot glass

Molten tin

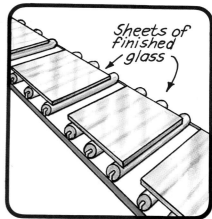

Sheets of finished glass

The molten glass is pulled out of the furnace. It is drawn through rollers to make it flat. It goes into another furnace and floats on hot liquid tin. As it moves across the tin, it cools and becomes harder.

After it has cooled down still more, the glass is hard and smooth and ready to be cut to the right size

How bottles are made

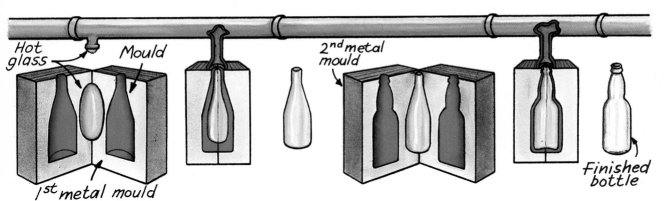

Hot glass

Mould

2nd metal mould

1st metal mould

Finished bottle

1 Molten glass from the furnace goes into a metal mould. The mould is shaped roughly like two halves of a bottle.

2 The mould closes and air is blown in. The air pushes the glass against the side of the mould. This makes it roughly bottle-shaped.

3 The glass goes into a second mould shaped like a finished bottle. The mould closes. Air is blown in and makes the bottle.

Glass blowing

Furnace

Some bottles and vases are still made by people and not by machines. They blow into a hot blob of molten glass. The glass can be turned on the end of a long pipe and blown into the right shapes.

How mirrors work

Protective paint

Glass   Metal

A mirror is a piece of glass that has been painted on one side with shiny metal. Underneath the silvery paint is a coat of protective paint.

Soap and washing machines

What soap does to water

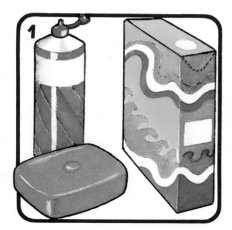

Soap is made up of millions of tiny parts called molecules. They are much too small to see.

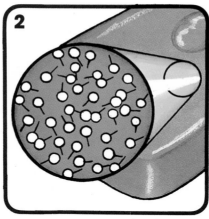

Each molecule has one part, the head, which loves water and another, the tail, which hates it.

When you put dirty clothes into soapy water, the tails stick to the dirt to get away from the water.

The tails pull the dirt away from the cloth. This makes the cloth clean and the water dirty.

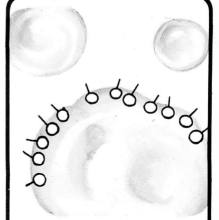

The tails of the soap molecules try to get out of the water. They break up the drops of water.

As the soapy water is broken up, it spreads out. Water without soap stays in drops.

Soap test

Do this simple test to see how soap changes water.

Dip a pencil in some clean water. Shake the drops onto a plate. Now dip the pencil in some soapy water and shake the drops onto another plate.

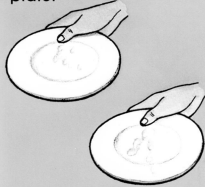

Tip the plates a little and you will see that the clean water stays in drops and the soapy water spreads out.

How a washing machine works

When you turn on a washing machine, water goes into the drum and mixes with soap powder. The clothes spin round in the hot soapy water. This takes out the dirt.

Hot and cold water goes into the machine through these pipes at the back. The dirty water goes out through the big grey pipes at the bottom.

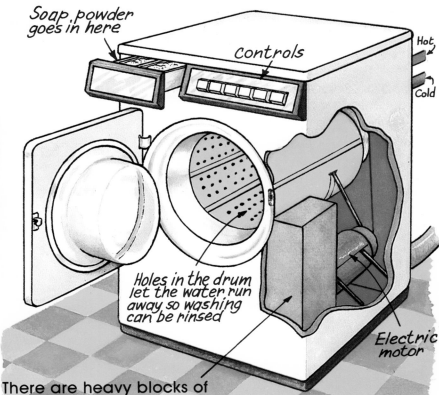

Soap powder goes in here

Controls

Hot

Cold

Holes in the drum let the water run away so washing can be rinsed

Electric motor

There are heavy blocks of concrete inside the machine. These stop it jumping about when the drum spins round very fast.

An electric motor drives a belt that is attached to a large wheel at the back of the drum. This makes the drum spin round.

How a cassette recorder works

The picture below shows a cassette tape recorder. Part of it has been cut away so you can see how it works.

This is the electric motor. It takes electricity from the batteries and makes the spindles go round so the tape goes past the tape head.

The batteries are kept in here. They store electricity that is needed for the motor, microphone and loudspeaker.

You do not need batteries if the recorder can be plugged into the electricity.

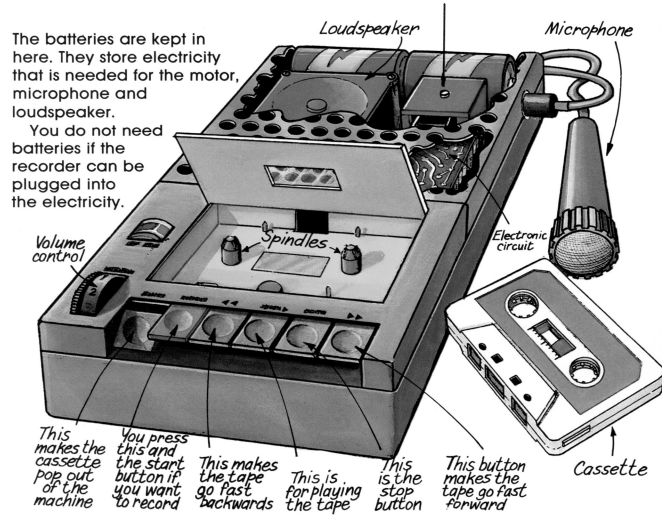

Loudspeaker

Microphone

Volume control

Spindles

Electronic circuit

This makes the cassette pop out of the machine

You press this and the start button if you want to record

This makes the tape go fast backwards

This is for playing the tape

This is the stop button

This button makes the tape go fast forward

Cassette

Two spools

Tape passes behind this window

There are two spools in a cassette. When the recorder is going, tape winds from one spool to the other.

Tiny magnets on the tape

The plastic tape is covered with thousands of tiny magnets that are too small to see.

Tape head pushes against the tape

When you play the tape, the magnets make electric signals in the tape head as they move past.

The electronic circuit sends electric signals to and from the tape head.

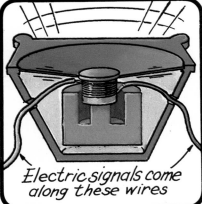

Electric signals come along these wires

The loudspeaker changes electric signals into the sounds of voices and music. This is what you hear.

Your voice makes part of the microphone shake

When you speak into the microphone, it turns your voice into an electric signal.

How this book was made

First we discussed what to write about. Then we researched and wrote about the different things.

Next we decided where the words and pictures should go. The designer drew rough plans for each page.

The drawings and the words were shown to children to make sure they could understand them.

Then the drawings were sent to an artist. She painted the pictures you can see in the book.

The words were sent to be typeset. This makes them easier to read than words from a typewriter.

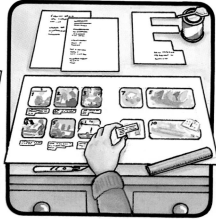

The typeset words were stuck down around the pictures. The complete pages were then sent to the printers.

At the printers

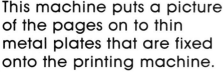

This machine puts a picture of the pages on to thin metal plates that are fixed onto the printing machine.

Colour books are actually printed with only four different colours—black, blue, red and yellow. Each sheet of paper is printed four times with a different printing plate for each colour.

Look carefully at a colour picture in a book. It is made up of lots of tiny dots of ink.

The sheets of printed paper are folded so the pages are in the right order. They are cut to size and go on to a binding machine. This staples, sews or glues the pages together. Small books can have their covers stapled on. Some books have covers glued on.

Index

©1981 Usborne Publishing Ltd.

First published in 1981 by Usborne Publishing Ltd, 20 Garrick Street, London WC2E 9BJ

The type was set in Avant Garde by F. J. Milner & Sons Ltd, Brentford, Middlesex

The name Usborne and the device are Trade Marks of Usborne Publishing Ltd.

Printed in Belgium by Henri Proost et Cie, Turnhout, Belgium